Chapter 1

Barbie peered out the airplane window. Below, she saw an island covered with palm trees. The crystal blue ocean shimmered around it. Barbie grinned at her sisters—Skipper, Stacie, and Chelsea. They were traveling to the tropical island so Chelsea could compete in a dance competition.

"Can you see the beach where my

competition will take place?" Chelsea asked.

"Everything looks like ants from up here!" Stacie replied.

Skipper clutched her stomach. "When is this thing going to land?" she moaned.

By each of the girls' seats, four cuddly

ADAPTED BY MOLLY MCGUIRE WOODS

BASED ON THE ORIGINAL SCREENPLAY BY
AMY WOLFRAM AND KACEY ARNOLD

ILLUSTRATED BY PATRICK IAN MOSS AND
THE ARTFUL DOODLERS

RANDOM HOUSE  NEW YORK

Special thanks to Ryan Ferguson, Debra Mostow Zakarin, Kristine Lombardi, Rita Lichtwardt, Nicole Corse, Karen Painter, Stuart Smith, Sammie Suchland, Charnita Belcher, Julia Phelps, Julia Pistor, Renata Marchand, Michelle Cogan, and Kris Fogel

Published in the United States by Random House Children's Books, a division of Penguin Random House LLC, 1745 Broadway, New York, NY 10019, and in Canada by Penguin Random House Canada Limited, Toronto.

Random House and the colophon are registered trademarks of Penguin Random House LLC.

ISBN 978-0-399-55136-9 (trade) — ISBN 978-0-399-55137-6 (lib. bdg.) — ISBN 978-0-399-55138-3 (ebook)
randomhousekids.com
Printed in the United States of America
10 9 8 7 6 5 4 3 2

puppies wriggled in their carriers. Honey, Taffy, Rookie, and DJ were as excited as the girls to touch down on an island paradise.

"We will be on the ground shortly," the pilot announced.

Barbie couldn't wait to hang out on the beach with her sisters. Plus, she had a surprise for them.

A little while later, the plane landed. A woman wearing a necklace made of flowers greeted the girls. She placed a lei just like hers around each girl's neck. Then she tucked a flower behind each puppy's ear.

"My flower looks like a firework!" Rookie barked.

Honey barked her approval. *"Taffy, your pink flower matches your collar!"*

Taffy wagged her tail. She barked at DJ, who looked like he was about to sneeze. *"Don't you like your flower, DJ?"*

"I think I'm a-a-al-lergic!" DJ replied. Then he sneezed.

"Adorable as always," Barbie chuckled, watching the puppies. To her, they were just barking and playing; she and her sisters couldn't understand that they were talking. "Let's go see the surprise!"

"When?" asked Chelsea.

"Right now!" Barbie announced. "Who's ready for a quick road trip?"

Stacie frowned. "I want to snorkel and surf. The hotel suggested signing up right away."

"I have to practice my routine," Chelsea protested. "We're here for my dance competition, remember?"

"And I have to update my blog," Skipper added.

This was not how Barbie thought her sisters would react. "Guys," she urged.

"We have plenty of time! You're going to love this. I promise."

Just then, Chelsea's rival Lindsey twirled by. "Hi, Chelsea. See you at the competition tomorrow," she said.

"See?" Chelsea pleaded. "I need as much rehearsal time as possible to compete with her!"

"You'll be able to rehearse after the surprise," Barbie reassured her little sister.

Chelsea didn't look convinced. "What if we're late getting back?" she asked.

"It's a small island. How long could

it take?" Barbie replied. She knew her sisters would have fun once they were there. Besides, what could go wrong? She walked over to the rental car counter. She introduced herself to the woman standing behind it and asked to rent a car.

"Call me Auntie Hannah," the friendly woman said. "All of our cars are booked. But I have just the thing for you." She pointed across the parking lot.

"A golf cart?" Chelsea groaned.

"Perfect!" Barbie squealed. "We'll only need our backpacks for the day, anyway."

The sisters climbed into the tiny golf cart. The puppies piled into the rear compartment.

"*Whee!*" Honey cried. "*We get to go backward!*"

Barbie grinned. It was time to have some fun! She stepped on the gas.

Chapter 2

"The surprise is next to the island's famous banyan tree arch," Barbie explained as she drove. She couldn't wait until the girls found out that they were going to the island's Dancing Horse Festival!

Stacie perked up. "I read about a hiking path that goes right through the banyan tree arch."

Skipper whipped out her cell phone. "I'll use my GPS for directions." She stuck her arm out of the golf cart. She wiggled it in every direction. "No reception," she said, frowning.

Stacie and Chelsea tried their phones. Neither one had any signal at all.

"How are we going to get there without GPS?" Skipper wondered.

"Maybe we should just head back to the hotel," Chelsea grumbled.

But Barbie wasn't worried. "There's only one road around the island. It can't be that hard to find the festival!"

The girls drove through the rain forest. Eventually Barbie pointed at a giant spindly tree. A tunnel ran through its middle. It was big enough to walk through. "Look!" she exclaimed. "The banyan tree arch!"

"Forget the tree, are those dancing

horses?" Chelsea asked excitedly. "Cool!"

"I knew you guys would like it," Barbie said. "I mean, they're dancing horses!"

Barbie pulled into a parking area. She parked next to an SUV with a horse trailer attached to it.

The girls and puppies made their way through the crowd to the outdoor arena. The sisters took their seats. The puppies played nearby. The show was about to begin in the center ring.

Music played and a horse trainer entered the ring. She led a brown, bright-eyed horse through its paces. "Beauty here is the youngest member of our dancing troupe," she explained into her microphone. Beauty paused, and Chelsea saw that she was nervous.

"You can do it, Beauty!" Chelsea shouted.

Beauty pranced around the ring.

"Beauty's mother, Silver, was our first champion," the trainer continued.

Barbie noticed Silver, a stunning dapple-gray mare, outside the ring.

"Next up is Beauty's sister, Spirit. Her rider is my brother, Marco."

Spirit began an amazing routine.

She pranced and high-stepped around the ring. She even hopped on her hind legs with Marco on her back! *Her name certainly fits her,* Barbie thought.

At the girls' feet, the puppies practiced high-stepping like the ponies. But when a

butterfly flew near, they decided to chase it instead.

"Look at me!" Rookie exclaimed, leaping after the butterfly. *"I'm a dancing horse!"*

"More like a falling pup," DJ joked.

The butterfly landed on Honey's nose. She looked at it cross-eyed. Then it fluttered toward the parking lot.

"There it is!" DJ exclaimed as the puppies gave chase.

"Wait for me!" Taffy called.

The puppies dashed after the butterfly without the girls noticing. They followed it to the SUV Barbie had parked next to.

The puppies pranced into the SUV after the butterfly. Then they stopped in their tracks.

"Whoa!" Honey exclaimed. *"What is this place?"* She began to sniff around.

The inside of the SUV was a puppy

paradise! There was a huge TV playing dog videos. There were doggy beds and tons of treats. There was even a doggy smoothie station.

The puppies made themselves at home, blending smoothies and getting cozy. It was a doggy dream!

Suddenly, a large white poodle entered. He frowned. *"Darlings, please,"* he said grouchily. *"All that racket is making my fur ache."*

The puppies froze. *"Sorry,"* they said.

"Do you live here?" Taffy asked.

The poodle nodded. *"This is my*

residence. I am Archibald the Third. I come from a champion line of Archibalds. I myself have won Best in Show four times."

The puppies listened as Archibald told them about his life on the road with the horses. It was so exciting—and the smoothies were so good—that they lost track of time.

When the show ended, Barbie and her sisters entered the ring. They chatted with the trainers, Vivian and Marco.

"We can see why you've won so many ribbons," Barbie said. "Do you train on the island?"

"Yes," Vivian said, "on the north side."

Chelsea tugged on Marco's shirt. "Do you have any tips for winning a *dance* competition?"

Marco thought for a moment. "Well, Spirit does most of the dancing. But you've got to feel the beat of the music and forget about the audience. Just remember to have fun."

"I'm all about fun!" Stacie added. "Any tips for the most fun beach?"

Marco nodded. "That would be at White Sands Campground. It's got everything—

swimming, surfing, snorkeling. We'll be staying there for the next few nights before heading home."

"Maybe we'll see you there!" Stacie said.

Marco and Vivian waved. They led their horses toward their trailer.

"Okay," Chelsea announced. "Back to the hotel. I've got twenty-six hours left until the competition."

Stacie was walking toward the parking lot. She stopped for a moment. "Wait. Where are the puppies?" she asked.

The girls looked around. Then Chelsea saw the puppies' heads through the

SUV's back window. But the SUV was

pulling away!

Chapter 3

"Is it me or are we moving?" Rookie exclaimed. The puppies looked out the back window and saw that the SUV was driving out of the parking lot—with the girls running after it!

Uh-oh.

"Come on!" Barbie called. "We can catch them."

The sisters leaped into their golf cart.

Barbie steered it toward the banyan tree arch. If she used the arch as a shortcut, they could catch up with the SUV. Barbie hoped their cart was narrow enough to make it through.

Screech! The golf cart scraped against the sides of the arch. It came to a stop. They were stuck!

"What are we going to do about the puppies?" Stacie asked.

Chelsea pointed to the setting sun. "We'll never make it back in time for me to rehearse tonight," she moaned.

Barbie frowned. She needed a plan.

"Stacie, do you remember the beach the trainers are going to?"

"White Sands Campground," Stacie replied.

"Right!" Barbie agreed. "That's where the puppies are headed. They'll be safe with Vivian and Marco tonight. But we should stay put for now. It's getting dark. We can hike out to the main road tomorrow to find help."

"We're going to *sleep* here?" Chelsea whined.

Barbie nodded. "It's not every day you can camp under the stars," she said, putting on a brave smile and wrapping her arm around Chelsea.

Meanwhile, the puppies looked out the window as the SUV pulled into White Sands Campground.

"It's dark out," Honey whispered.

"Barbie's not here. How is she going to sleep without me?" Taffy wondered aloud.

"Don't worry; it will wrinkle your fur," Archibald said. *"Your girls will find you in the morning. You will be safe here with us."*

The puppies huddled together.

"How long until tomorrow?" Honey asked.

Chapter 4

The girls settled under the banyan tree for the evening.

"I'm hungry. What's for dinner?" Chelsea asked.

Stacie dumped a pile of energy bars from her backpack.

"Auntie Hannah left some water and blankets under the seats," Barbie said, passing out the supplies.

The girls quietly munched for a bit. Barbie could tell her sisters were disappointed about the turn of events. She needed a way to cheer them up. "Do you remember the What-If game we used to play?"

Skipper, Stacie, and Chelsea nodded.

"We'd say 'what if' and then imagine something amazing," Barbie continued. "This seems like a great time to play. Why don't you start, Chelsea?"

The girls passed the evening imagining all sorts of wonderful things, like a camper with a slide and a swimming pool.

A strange bird cawed in the banyan tree above.

Chelsea leaped into Barbie's lap. "What was that?"

Barbie hugged her little sister. "It was probably just a macaw. The macaw parrot is the official bird of the island. There's even a legend about the Seven Macaw constellation." Barbie pointed to a group of stars in the sky.

"The native fishermen would use the constellation to help them find their way. Its beak points to the North Star," she explained to her sisters.

The sound of Barbie's voice was
soothing. Her sisters drifted to sleep as
the stars twinkled above.

Chapter 5

The next morning, Stacie pulled out more energy bars. "Breakfast?" she chirped.

The girls each took a bar.

Chelsea jumped up and down. "Twelve hours until the competition. But first we've got to save the puppies. Let's get moving, people!"

The girls snapped into action. They hiked down a path, which was very muddy from a recent rainstorm.

"We should be able to call for help from the main road," Barbie said.

Skipper pointed ahead. "Um . . . the main road is washed out."

Chelsea sighed.

"There has to be another way," said Barbie. She spied a mountain ahead. "There."

Skipper's mouth dropped open in shock. "We're going to hike *that*?"

The girls started to climb. The trail was challenging. "How much farther?" Chelsea asked.

Barbie scanned their surroundings for something to help with the climb. She saw a low-hanging vine. "This should hold us," she said. She showed the girls how to pull themselves up the mountainside using the vine. When they finally reached the top, Barbie gasped. "Look at the view!"

"I see some buildings," Stacie said, pointing down below.

"Looks like a village. Maybe someone there can help us," Barbie reasoned.

"There's just one problem," Skipper announced. She pointed at the steep path ahead of them. "How are we going to get to it?"

The girls split up to look for an easier way down.

Luckily, they discovered a zip line and helmets nearby. Each girl zip-lined from the top of the mountain into the village

below. Everyone but Skipper was excited.

"Let's get our cart stuck in a tree! Let's go down a rickety old zip line! Sister adventure? More like sister torture!" Skipper said as she reluctantly pushed down the zip line.

The sisters walked through the small village. Everything appeared to be closed.

Barbie frowned. Her sisters were counting on her for a way out of this mess. They needed to find the puppies *and* make it back in time for the dance competition! She wasn't sure she could pull it off. Then she noticed another rental car stand ahead. There was a familiar-looking woman standing behind the desk.

"Auntie Hannah?" Barbie called.

The woman smiled. "I see you've met my sister at the airport. I'm Auntie *Anna*."

Barbie grinned. "Do you have any cars available for rent? Our golf cart is stuck in the banyan tree arch."

Auntie Anna chuckled. "That happens a lot. I'll show you what I have." She motioned toward the lot behind her.

The girls turned and saw a sparkly pink deluxe camper. It looked like the one they had dreamed up during their

What-If game!

Skipper jumped up and down. "Auntie Anna, I could hug you!"

The girls borrowed a map and climbed into the fancy camper. Barbie revved the engine.

"The White Sands Campground is just past the cove," Auntie Anna explained.

"Thank you!" Barbie shouted as they drove away. "Puppies, here we come!"

Chapter 6

After a few wrong turns, the girls found a sign that read WHITE SANDS CAMPGROUND AHEAD.

"As soon as we pass the cove, we'll be there," Barbie said with relief.

The camper sputtered to a stop.

Barbie checked the dashboard. The gas gauge read E for empty.

Skipper and Chelsea moaned.

Barbie tried to look on the bright side. "Hey, the camper got us this far. We just need to find a way to the cove."

"Let me guess—parasailing? Hang gliding?" said Skipper, rolling her eyes.

"Well, those are a little extreme. Turning around should do the trick," said Stacie. The sisters turned to where Stacie was pointing. They were already at White Sands Beach!

"There's the SUV!" Chelsea said.

But there was no sign of the horses, trainers, or puppies. Where was everyone?

"They have to be here somewhere,"

Barbie said, looking in every direction.

"It doesn't matter," Chelsea said. She crossed her arms angrily. "Even if we find the puppies, we're probably going to miss my dance competition."

"It's going to be okay," Barbie replied.

"You keep saying that," Chelsea cried. "But what if it isn't? What if we came all this way and I don't even get to do my routine?"

"I know things haven't gone exactly as planned," Barbie said softly. "But no one can control what's going to happen all the time. Not even me."

"That stinks," Chelsea said.

"How about playing a different kind of What-If game?" Barbie suggested. "Instead of thinking of the most amazing thing that could happen, let's think of the most awful thing that could happen." She nudged Chelsea playfully. "I bet you'd be pretty good at the That Stinks game."

Chelsea smiled. It was worth a shot.

The sisters traded awful what-ifs for a few minutes, making each other laugh.

"What if a giant submarine came out of the water, and the captain told us we had to live underwater from now on?" Barbie started.

Chelsea giggled. "That would stink! Or what if a huge octopus-shark leaped out of the water and tried to eat us!"

"That would stink!" Barbie laughed. "What if the puppies became giants, and we were *their* pets?"

Chelsea snorted. Then she grew serious. "What if it takes so long to find them that I miss the chance to do my routine? Or what if I *do* my routine, but I mess up in front of everyone?"

Barbie put her arm around her youngest sister. "Just because you mess up doesn't mean you fail. Getting out there and doing your best is all that matters."

Chelsea gazed out at the ocean, thinking about Barbie's words. Then she pointed toward the waves. "What if the puppies learned to *surf*?"

In the distance, Barbie spied Rookie

and DJ. They wore snorkeling gear and were riding a wave on a surfboard!

Chelsea and Barbie raced to find Skipper and Stacie. Then they jogged down the beach.

All four puppies were surfing! They rode waves into the shore and raced toward the girls.

"Hang ten!" Rookie called.

The girls fell to the sand, and the puppies covered them with kisses.

"We knew you'd come!" Honey cried.

"Righteous waves, puppies!" Stacie said, laughing.

Barbie noticed Marco and Vivian standing nearby. "Thanks for taking care of the puppies," she said.

"I'm glad you made it. I was starting to worry," Vivian said.

"It took a little longer than we planned. Turns out shortcuts aren't always short," Barbie joked.

Vivian laughed. She turned to Chelsea. "Isn't your dance competition tonight?"

Chelsea nodded sadly. "But we don't have any way to get there."

"You do now!" Vivian offered. "Marco, round up the horses. Get everyone in the trailer."

The sisters, puppies, horses, and trainers piled into the SUV and trailer. With the sun setting, they were almost out of time. But they had to try!

Chapter 7

The SUV and trailer zipped along the main road. After a while, Vivian slowed to a stop and pointed ahead. "We're not going to be able to cross over the bridge," she said. "It's washed out. Looks like we won't make it in time for your dance competition after all, Chelsea."

"But we're so close," Chelsea replied disappointedly.

Marco said, "*We* can't take you across, but I think I know who *can*. . . ."

Moments later, the girls stood by the bridge with Beauty, Spirit, and Silver. The horses were harnessed and ready to finish the journey.

Barbie took the lead with Spirit. Chelsea climbed onto Beauty. Skipper and Stacie shared Silver. Marco gave them directions to the competition. Then he handed them the puppies.

"We'll meet you there. Remember to have fun," he said to Chelsea, and winked.

Barbie clicked her tongue and the

horses took off. The sisters held on to the puppies and hoped for the best.

Meanwhile, the puppies were excited for another adventure. *"Ride 'em, cowboy!"* Rookie exclaimed.

Chapter 8

The girls rode the horses for what seemed like forever.

Finally, Barbie said, "The competition has to be just over this hill." They were going to make it! But when they reached the hilltop, the girls saw the banyan tree arch—not the competition. They were turned around again!

"Now what?" Chelsea asked.

Barbie sighed. "I don't know," she admitted. "I'm sorry, Chelsea. You were right. We shouldn't have gone to the Dancing Horse Festival. Then none of this would have happened." Barbie hung her head. "I messed up. You guys count on me, and I don't always know what to do."

Chelsea had never seen her sister so sad, and tried to cheer her up. She repeated Barbie's own words. "Just because you mess up doesn't mean you fail."

Skipper, Stacie, and Chelsea gathered around Barbie. "You could have let us know how you were feeling," Stacie said.

"Yeah," said Chelsea. "You can tell us when you're worried. We're sisters."

"I'm sorry I ruined our trip," Barbie said.

"You know," Stacie offered, "if it wasn't for the things that happened, we never would have had this adventure together."

"It *was* kind of fun," Skipper added.

"Really?" Barbie asked, perking up.

The sisters nodded. Missing the competition was disappointing, but the important thing was that they were together.

Chelsea looked at the sky. "I guess

we're camping under the stars for another night."

Barbie snapped her fingers. "That's it!" she cried. "The stars!"

Her sisters looked confused.

"The competition is north. The Seven Macaw constellation *points* north! We can follow the constellation just like the native fishermen used it to find their way home."

The girls steered their horses north to follow the stars!

Chapter 9

A short ride later, Chelsea pulled Beauty to a stop. Chelsea heard her name over the loudspeaker followed by an announcement.

"We have waited as long as we can. The trophy goes to . . . ," the announcer began.

"Wait! I'm here!" Chelsea called, rushing backstage. She ran into the announcer, Auntie Savannah. She was

Anna and Hannah's sister and looked exactly like them.

"I'm terribly sorry, but you're too late. I'm about to announce the winner," said Auntie Savannah. The puppies looked up at her with their sad puppy eyes, and Auntie Savannah couldn't resist. Chelsea would get to perform her routine!

The stage lights dimmed. Chelsea locked eyes with Barbie. "What if I really mess up in front of everyone?"

Barbie smiled. "As long as you try your best, you can't fail."

Chelsea took a deep breath. She

walked onstage. She saw Beauty and the other horses in the outdoor crowd. When the music swelled, Chelsea began her routine. She spun and twirled. Then she took a running start for her first big leap. But instead of nailing the move, she fell! She landed on her hip with a crash. If only she'd had more time to practice.

The whole audience waited to see what she would do next.

Chelsea stood and smoothed her skirt. She locked eyes with Beauty in the crowd. Then she had an idea. "Hey, Beauty!" she called. "I could really use a partner!"

Beauty leaped onstage. She pranced next to Chelsea, performing her own routine. Chelsea followed Beauty's lead. Next, Spirit took the stage with Barbie on her back. They strutted and high-stepped to the music. Then the puppies leaped onstage.

"*Gonna get my groove on!*" DJ exclaimed.

In the crowd, Stacie turned to Skipper. "What should we do?" she asked.

"Dance!" Skipper cried.

The girls joined their sisters onstage.

The horses, puppies, and girls grooved to the music behind Chelsea. Chelsea remembered Marco's advice to feel the beat and have fun. *I can do that,* she thought. She twirled and freestyled her way across the floor. The music swelled. Chelsea made one last spin across the stage. She landed in a split and threw her arms in the air. The crowd went wild.

Chelsea beamed. Now, *that* was fun!

A few moments later, all the dance competitors—including Chelsea's rival, Lindsey—lined up onstage. It was time to announce the winner. Chelsea had heard from the other dancers that Lindsey was sure to win.

Auntie Savannah wheeled out a giant trophy. "Our winner is . . . Lindsey!"

Chelsea and the other dancers clapped.

But Lindsey put up her hands in protest. "I can't accept it," she said. "Chelsea had dancing horses and cute puppies! She was amazing!"

Chelsea blushed. "I'm just glad I got a chance to perform."

Lindsey pushed the trophy toward her anyway. "Don't worry," Lindsey said with a smile. "I plan on winning it back at the next competition."

Chelsea grinned. She took the trophy. It had been a long journey, and she had wanted to give up. But her sisters had helped her through.

"I couldn't have done it without Barbie, Skipper, and Stacie," she said, motioning toward them. "And Beauty, Spirit, and

Silver. And Honey, DJ, Rookie, and Taffy. And Vivian and Marco," Chelsea added, seeing her friends in the crowd. "And the aunties," she continued, eyeing Aunties Savannah, Hannah, and Anna in the crowd.

Lindsey interrupted Chelsea's thank-you speech. "Now show me those moves!" she cried, throwing an arm over Chelsea's shoulder. The crowd cheered as the music began.

Everyone danced. Chelsea looked at the stars, glowing brightly above her. Barbie had been right. Things didn't always go as planned. In fact, sometimes things went wildly wrong. But the important thing was to never stop trying. There was nothing she and her sisters couldn't do if they worked hard and relied on each other. And for that, she thanked her lucky stars.